A Break-of-Day Book

Ever since 1928, when Wanda Gág's classic *Millions of Cats* appeared, Coward-McCann has been publishing books of high quality for young readers. Among them are the easy-to-read stories known as Break-of-Day books. This series appears under the colophon shown above — a rooster crowing in the sunrise — which is adapted from one of Wanda Gág's illustrations for *Tales from Grimm*.

Though the language used in Break-of-Day books is deliberately kept as clear and as simple as possible, the stories are not written in a controlled vocabulary. And while chosen to be within the grasp of readers in the primary grades, their content is far-ranging and varied enough to captivate children who have just begun crossing the momentous threshold into the world of books.

Nate the Great
and the
Missing Key

by
Marjorie Weinman Sharmat
illustrations by Marc Simont

Coward-McCann, Inc. New York

Library of Congress Cataloging-in Publication Data
Sharmat, Marjorie Weinman.   Nate the Great and the
missing key. (A Break-of-day book)   SUMMARY: Nate the
Great and his dog Sludge look for Annie's housekey which
has mysteriously disappeared.   [1. Lost and found posses-
sions.   2. Mystery and detective stories]   I. Simont, Marc.
II. Title.   PZ7.S5299Naug   [E]   80-13952
ISBN 0-698-20630-4
10   9   8   7

To Mitch,
with love and thanks
for giving me the key
to this mystery

M.W.S.

I, Nate the Great,
am a detective.
I am not afraid of anything.
Except for one thing.
Today I am going
to a birthday party
for the one thing
I am afraid of.
Annie's dog Fang.

This morning my dog Sludge

and I were getting ready

for the party.

The doorbell rang.

I opened the door.

Annie and Fang were standing there.

Fang looked bigger than ever

and so did his teeth.

But he looked like a birthday dog.

He was wearing a stupid sweater

and a new collar.

"I need help," Annie said.

"I can't find the key to my house.

So I can't get inside

to have the birthday party

for Fang."

I, Nate the Great,
was sorry about the key
and glad about the party.
I said,
"Tell me about your key."
"Well," Annie said,

"the last time I saw it
was when I went out
to get Fang a birthday surprise
to eat."
"To eat?" I said.
"Yes," Annie said.

"Some surprise food.
It's the one present
I had forgotten to buy.
I got Fang lots of presents.
A striped sweater.
And a new collar
with a license number,
a name tag,
a little silver dog dish,
and a little silver bone
to hang from the collar.
See how pretty Fang looks
and hear how nicely he jingles."
I, Nate the Great,
did not want
to look at Fang

or listen to him.

"Tell me more," I said.

"Well, Rosamond and her four cats
were at my house," Annie said.

"She was helping me
get ready for the party.

When I went to the store,
I left Rosamond and the cats
in my house.
I left Fang in the yard.
I left the key to my house
on a table.
That is the last time
I saw the key.
When I got back,
Fang was still in the yard.
But the house was locked,
and Rosamond and her cats
were gone.
Rosamond left this note
stuck to my front door."

Your Key Can Be Found
At A Place That Is Round
A Place That Is Safe
And where Things Are Shiny.
A Place That Is Big
Because It's Not Tiny.
And This Is A Poem.
And I went Home.

"That is a strange poem,"

I said.

"Sometimes Rosamond is strange,"

Annie said.

I, Nate the Great,

already knew that.

16

"You must go
to Rosamond's house
and ask her
where she put your key," I said.
"I went to her house,"
Annie said. "But it was locked, too.
I rang the bell, but no one was home."
"This is a big day
for Rosamond
and locked doors," I said.
"Who else has a key
to your house?"
"My mother and father.
But they went out for the day.
They don't like dog parties,"
Annie said.

I, Nate the Great,

knew that dog parties

are very easy not to like.

But I said,

"I will take your case."

I wrote a note to my mother.

Dear mother,
I am on a case.
I am looking for a round, safe,
shiny, big place.
I do not know where or what
a round, safe, shiny, big place is
But when I find it
I will be back.
Love,
Nate the Great

Annie, Fang, Sludge, and I
went to
Annie's house.
"What does your key look like?"
I asked.

"It is silver and shiny,"
Annie said.
Sludge and I looked around.
There were many places
to leave a key.
Under Annie's doormat.
In her flower garden.
Up her drainpipe.
In her mailbox.
But they were not round,
safe, shiny, and big.
"I will have to look
in other places," I said.

"Fang and I will wait
for you here," Annie said.
I, Nate the Great,
was glad to hear that.
Sludge and I went to Oliver's house.
Oliver is a pest.
But I had a case to solve.
I had a job to do.
I knew that Oliver
collects shiny things.
Like tin cans, safety pins,
badges, poison ivy,
and pictures of the sun.
Each week he collects
one new shiny thing.
Perhaps this week

it was a key.

"Did Rosamond leave a shiny key
with you in a big, round, safe place?"
I asked.

"No," Oliver said.

"This is not my key week.
This is my week
for shiny eels.
Would you like to see
my new eel?"
I, Nate the Great,
did not want to see
a new eel
or an old eel.
I started to leave.

"May I follow you?"

Oliver asked.

"No," I said.

"I will help you look

for the key," Oliver said.

"All right," I said.

"When I go east,

you go west.

When I go south,

you go north."

"But we won't be together,"

Oliver said.

"Exactly," I said.

Sludge and I left Oliver's house.

I did not look back.

I knew what I would see.

Oliver.

I, Nate the Great,
was busy thinking
and looking.
All at once I saw
a big, safe place.
A bank.
I knew there were many
round, shiny things
in a bank.

Like pennies

and nickels

and dimes

and quarters.

Sludge and I walked inside.

Oliver followed us.

Sludge and I looked
on desks and behind counters.
Then we crawled on the floor.
If Rosamond had been here,
there would be cat hairs
all over the floor.

I saw paper clips
and a broken pen
and a penny
and mud.
And a bank guard.
First his feet.
Then the rest of him.
"Do you want
to make a deposit?" he asked.
I, Nate the Great,
wished I could deposit Oliver
in the bank.
I said, "Did anyone strange
with four cats
leave a key here?"
The guard pointed to the door.

Sludge and I left.

Now I, Nate the Great,

knew where I should *not* look

for the key.

A bank was not

a strange enough place

for a strange person like Rosamond

to leave a key.

I had to think of a strange place.

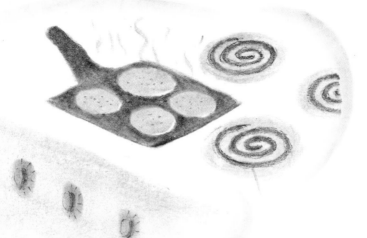

I thought of a kitchen
with bottles of syrup,
hunks of butter,
and stacks of pancakes.
It was not a strange place.
But it was a good place
to think of
because I, Nate the Great,
was hungry.
It was time for lunch.
Sludge and I started for home.

I felt something breathing
on the back of my neck.
I turned around.
It was Oliver.

"I will follow you forever,"
Oliver said.
I, Nate the Great,
knew that forever
was far too long
to be followed
by Oliver.

Sludge and I started to run.

We ran down the street,

up a hill,

around five corners,

and into an alley.

We lost Oliver.

I sat down to rest

beside a garbage can.

Sludge sniffed it.

Sludge likes garbage cans.

I stared at the can.

I had an idea.

A garbage can

would be a perfect place

for Rosamond to hide a key!

It was big and round and shiny

with a shiny cover and shiny handles.
It was safe because no one
would look inside a garbage can.
Except Sludge.
And it was a very strange place
for a key.

Strange enough for Rosamond.
There were not
many places like that.
Now I, Nate the Great,
knew that I had to look
in Annie's garbage can.

Sludge and I walked

to the garbage can

behind Annie's house.

We bent low.

I did not want Annie

to see me

until I found the key

in her garbage can.

Then I would surprise her.

I tried to pull up the cover.

Sludge tried to push up the cover

with his nose.

I pulled harder.

Sludge pushed harder.

The cover came off.

We looked inside the can.

It was empty.

I, Nate the Great,

had not solved the case.

Sludge and I slunk home.

I was very hungry.

I gave Sludge a bone.

I made many pancakes.

I sat down to eat them.

But I did not have a fork.

I opened a drawer.

It was full of spoons and knives

and forks all together

in a shiny silver pile.

I had to pick up

many spoons and knives

before I found a fork.

It is hard to find something

silver and shiny

when it is mixed in

with other things

that are silver and shiny.

I, Nate the Great,

thought about that.

Maybe Annie's key was someplace

where nobody would *see* it

because it was with other

shiny silver things.

A strange place.

A round place.

A big place.

A safe place.

And now I, Nate the Great,

knew the place!

Sludge and I went back

to Annie's house.

Annie was sitting in front

with Fang.

She looked sad.

Fang looked big.

I ran up to Annie.

"I know where your key is,"

I said.

"Where?" Annie asked.

"Look at Fang's collar,"
I said.

Annie looked.

"I see Fang's name tag
hanging from his collar,"
she said. "And his license.
And his silver dog dish.
And his silver bone

41

and——————————my key!"

"Yes," I said. "I, Nate the Great,

say that Rosamond hung your key

from Fang's collar.

We did not notice it

because there were other

silver things there."

"But why did Rosamond

hang it there?"

Annie asked.

"Well, it is a very strange place,"

I said. "And remember Rosamond's poem.

A *round* place.

A *big* and *safe* place

where things are shiny.

Well, Fang's collar is round.

The things hanging from it

are shiny.

Fang is big.

And safe.

There is no place

more safe

to leave a key

than a few inches

from Fang's teeth.

No one would try

to take off that key.

Including me."

I started to leave.

"Wait!" Annie said.

She took the key

from Fang's collar.

"Now I can have my party

and you can come!"

I, Nate the Great,
was glad for Annie
and sorry for me.
Just then Rosamond
and her four cats
came up the walk.
"You found the key!"
she said. "I knew
I left it in the perfect place."

I, Nate the Great,

had many things

to say to Rosamond.

But the party was starting.

Annie unlocked the door.

We all went inside.

We sat around the birthday table.

Annie gave me

the seat of honor

because I had solved the case.

It was next to Fang.

I, Nate the Great,

hoped it would be

a very short party.